To R.T.

Text copyright © 1991 Kate Sinnett
Illustrations © 1991 Anthony Lewis
First published 1991 by Blackie and Son Ltd

A CIP catalogue record for this book is available
from the British Library

ISBN 0-216-93014-6

Blackie and Son Ltd
7 Leicester Place
London WC2H 7BP

First American edition published in 1991 by
Peter Bedrick Books
2112 Broadway
New York, NY 10023

Library of Congress
Cataloging-in-Publication Data

Sinnett, Kate
My five disguises / Kate Sinnett & Anthony Lewis.
— 1st American ed.
Summary: Playing at home, Joe surprises his
mother with a series of disguises.
ISBN 0-87226-444-0
[1,, Costume—Fiction. 2. Play—Fiction] I.
Lewis, Anthony.
1966- Ill II. Title
PZ7.S6184My 1991
[E]—dc20   90-44374
                                      CIP
                                      AC
ISBN 0-87226-444-0

10 9 8 7 6 5 4 3 2 1

Printed in Hong Kong

MY FIVE DISGUISES

KATE SINNETT AND ANTHONY LEWIS

BEDRICK · BLACKIE · NEW YORK

BLACKIE · LONDON

Joe was dressing up while his mother made the
supper. He found a big fur hat that almost came
over his eyes, and a shaggy woolly jacket with
sleeves much too long for him. He ran past the
cupboard he didn't like and downstairs.

'Growl, growl, I'm a bear. Growl, growl, I'm a
bear,' he growled, as he prowled along the hall and
into the kitchen.

'Help, help! A *bear*!' cried his mother, leaping onto a chair and waving a wooden spoon. 'Help! Joe! Rescue!'

'It's *me*!' said Joe.

His mother climbed down and hugged him. 'Oh, thank goodness, so it is. I thought it was a bear,' she said.

Joe went upstairs again. This time he found some old purple trousers. He tried to put them on, but they were much too long, so he tied the legs round his neck instead.

Then he put a bit of scarlet ribbon round his head. He scuttled downstairs again.

'Tootle-too! Tootle-ootle-ooo! Here comes the king!'
he trumpeted through the hall and into the kitchen.
    His mother curtseyed low and flourished a tea-towel.
    'Good afternoon, Your Majesty,' she said. 'Would
Your Majesty . . . um . . . care for some humble tea?'

'It's *me*!' said Joe.

'Oh...I'm so glad,' said his mother. 'I couldn't think of much to say to a king.'

Joe rushed upstairs again. This time he found a
long silky green shawl. He rolled himself up in it
and wriggled along.

'Splash, splish! I'm a fish,' he gurgled as he
flapped along the floor.

'A fish. Get back to the river! You'll die,' cried his mother, picking him up and running to the sink.

'But it's *me*!' said Joe, struggling.
'So it is!' said his mother, putting him down.
'What a relief. I thought it was a fish.'

Up went Joe again. He searched for a long time in
the dressing-up box. Then he put on several things
– hats, coats, gloves, scarves and his father's boots.
He found a rope and tied it round his middle.

He slithered down the stairs, and struggled through the rocky hall and up to the summit of the kitchen table.

'What a climb, mountaineer,' said his mother.
'Shall the rescue helicopter lift you down?' And she
picked him off the table.

'It's *me*!' said Joe.

'Oh, so it is,' said his mother. 'I thought it was a brave mountain climber.'

It was tough work getting back up the steep stair-mountain, but Joe managed it. He felt very hot in all the coats, so he thought he wouldn't wear so much this time. He wanted to feel cool and floaty. What could he be?

Not a clown – too jumpy. Not a slug – too fat and slimy. Not a baker – too sticky.

He found some long filmy bits of stuff; pale blue, green and pink. He tucked the ends round his shoulders, so the stuff hung down and floated out when he moved, like clouds.

The dancer drifted into the kitchen and all the spotlights shone on him. Roses and carnations fell at his feet.

'Encore! great dancer,' cried his mother, clapping and stamping her feet.

'It's *me*!' said Joe, jumping up and down.

'Good heavens! So it is,' said his mother. 'Well, supper's ready now. Who's going to eat it? Bear, or King, or Fish, or Mountaineer, or Dancer?'

'ALL of them!' said Joe.

Which explains why, by the time Joe's father came home, there was no apple pie left at all.